Dear Parent:
Your child's love of reading starts here!

Every child learns to read in a different way and at his or her own speed. Some go back and forth between reading levels and read favorite books again and again. Others read through each level in order. You can help your young reader improve and become more confident by encouraging his or her own interests and abilities. From books your child reads with you to the first books he or she reads alone, there are I Can Read Books for every stage of reading:

SHARED READING
Basic language, word repetition, and whimsical illustrations, ideal for sharing with your emergent reader

BEGINNING READING
Short sentences, familiar words, and simple concepts for children eager to read on their own

READING WITH HELP
Engaging stories, longer sentences, and language play for developing readers

READING ALONE
Complex plots, challenging vocabulary, and high-interest topics for the independent reader

ADVANCED READING
Short paragraphs, chapters, and exciting themes for the perfect bridge to chapter books

I Can Read Books have introduced children to the joy of reading since 1957. Featuring award-winning authors and illustrators and a fabulous cast of beloved characters, I Can Read Books set the standard for beginning readers.

A lifetime of discovery begins with the magical words "I Can Read!"

Visit www.icanread.com for information
on enriching your child's reading experience.

For Chris and Mara, who never *sleep*
—H. P.

For Rose–thanks for having it at your house!
—L. A.

Gouache and black pencil were used to prepare the full-color art.

I Can Read Book® is a trademark of HarperCollins Publishers.

Amelia Bedelia is a registered trademark of Peppermint Partners, LLC.

www.icanread.com

Library of Congress Cataloging-in-Publication Data

Parish, Herman.

Amelia Bedelia sleeps over / by Herman Parish ; pictures by Lynne Avril.

  p. cm.—(I can read! 1-beginning reading)

"Greenwillow Books."

Summary: Amelia Bedelia has a wonderful time at her first slumber party.

ISBN 978-0-06-209524-4 (trade ed.)—ISBN 978-0-06-209523-7 (pbk.) [1. Sleepovers—Fiction. 2. Humorous stories.]

I. Avril, Lynne,(date) ill. II. Title. PZ7.P2185Aps 2012 [Fic]—dc23 2012006186

12 13 14 15 16 SCP 10 9 8 7 6 5 4 3 2 1 First Edition

 Greenwillow Books

I Can Read!

BEGINNING
1
READING

Amelia Bedelia
· Sleeps Over ·

by **Herman Parish** ❋ pictures by **Lynne Avril**

Greenwillow Books, *An Imprint of* HarperCollins*Publishers*

Amelia Bedelia was excited.

Tonight was her very first sleepover.

All the girls in her class

were going to Rose's house

for a slumber party.

Amelia Bedelia and her mother

drove to Rose's house.

"Is a slumber party fun?"

asked Amelia Bedelia.

"Because sleeping is boring."

"You might not sleep much,"

said her mother.

"You will play, eat pizza, paint nails . . ."

"Do we paint the nails
and then hammer them?"
asked Amelia Bedelia.

"Or do we hammer them first?"

Amelia Bedelia's mother laughed.

"You'll have fun, sweetie," she said.

"I promise."

When Amelia Bedelia arrived,

the front door swung open.

Her friends ran out to greet her.

Rose's mother came outside, too.

"Good luck," said Amelia Bedelia's mom.

"I think I'll need it!" said Rose's mother.

"I am a light sleeper."

"Me too," said Amelia Bedelia.

She reached into her backpack

and pulled out her flashlight.

"I sleep with this light every night."

The girls played board games.
Amelia Bedelia had worried
that she would be bored,
but she was not.

Next, everyone went outside
and played tag
until the sun began to set.

"The pizza is here!"
called Rose's father.
"Come and get it!"

"And for dessert," said Rose's mother,
"we will toast marshmallows
and make s'mores."

"Won't that wreck your toaster?"
asked Amelia Bedelia.

"Marshmallows melt into gooey, blobby . . ."

Rose's father laughed.

"We'll toast them on the grill," he said.

15

After the pizza was gone,

Dawn speared a marshmallow

on Amelia Bedelia's stick.

Holly showed her how to turn it

carefully and slowly

to get a crunchy brown skin.

Amelia Bedelia put her marshmallow

on top of a chocolate bar

between two graham crackers.

"Yum!" said Amelia Bedelia.

"I'd like some more, please!"

"Now you know why

they're called s'mores!" said Rose.

After many more s'mores,

the girls went inside the house.

They put on their pajamas,

but it was not time to slumber yet.

Rose brought out bottles

of glittery nail polish

in more colors than the rainbow.

Every color had the perfect name.

Heather painted
Amelia Bedelia's nails

with "Shamrock Green" on her left hand,

"Blue Iceberg" on her right hand,

and "Banana Sunrise" on her right foot.

20

She saved her left foot for "Cotton Candy Cupcake."

Amelia Bedelia sighed and said,
"I'm so happy
we don't have to hammer them!"

21

Too soon, the clock struck ten.

"Bedtime, girls!" said Rose's mother.

"Lights out, and no giggling allowed!"

Oh well, thought Amelia Bedelia.

Here comes the slumber part

of this slumber party.

Off went the lights and lamps.

On went Amelia Bedelia's flashlight.

She showed her friends how to make

shadow puppets on the wall.

One by one,

the girls fell asleep.

All except Amelia Bedelia.

She was not one bit sleepy.

She made a rabbit.

 Then a barking dog.

Then an elephant

with a trunk to grab . . .

Oops!

Her flashlight went out.

"Oh, no," said Amelia Bedelia.

What light would keep her company now?

Then Amelia Bedelia noticed

a very bright light

peeking into the family room.

She pulled back the curtains.

A full moon shone down on her.

Now there was too much light!

Amelia Bedelia dragged her sleeping bag under Rose's Ping-Pong table.

Perfect, thought Amelia Bedelia.
Now I am having a sleepover
and a sleep under.

Amelia Bedelia snuggled down
into her cozy sleeping bag.
She gazed up at the moon.
She had heard people say that
there was a man in the moon.
She'd never seen him, until tonight.

He looked just like her dad.

Amelia Bedelia closed her eyes.

A second later, she was sound asleep.

The next morning,

the girls had a pillow fight.

Then they made chocolate chip pancakes

and helped to clean up the mess.

Amelia Bedelia's dad picked her up.

"Nice nails," said her father.

"Thanks, moon man," said Amelia Bedelia.

"Huh?" said her father.

"You sound like you need to take a nap."

And so Amelia Bedelia did,

all the way home.